DRAGON SLAYERS ACADEMY™ 19

# LITTLE GIANT—BIG TROUBLE

### By Kate McMullan
### Illustrated by Bill Basso

**GROSSET & DUNLAP**

For Caleb Lee Stiawalt in Iowa.—K.M.

For our first grandchildren, twins, Marco
and Stefano, with much love.—B.B

GROSSET & DUNLAP
Published by the Penguin Group
Penguin Group (USA) Inc., 375 Hudson Street, New York, New York 10014, U.S.A.
Penguin Group (Canada), 90 Eglinton Avenue East, Suite 700, Toronto, Ontario,
Canada M4P 2Y3 (a division of Pearson Penguin Canada Inc.)
Penguin Books Ltd, 80 Strand, London WC2R 0RL, England
Penguin Ireland, 25 St Stephen's Green, Dublin 2, Ireland
(a division of Penguin Books Ltd)
Penguin Group (Australia), 250 Camberwell Road, Camberwell,
Victoria 3124, Australia (a division of Pearson Australia Group Pty Ltd)
Penguin Books India Pvt Ltd, 11 Community Centre, Panchsheel Park,
New Delhi—110 017, India
Penguin Group (NZ), 67 Apollo Drive, Mairangi Bay,
Auckland 1311, New Zealand (a division of Pearson New Zealand Ltd)
Penguin Books (South Africa) (Pty) Ltd, 24 Sturdee Avenue, Rosebank,
Johannesburg 2196, South Africa

Penguin Books Ltd, Registered Offices:
80 Strand, London WC2R 0RL, England

Text copyright © 2007 by Kate McMullan. Illustrations copyright © 2007 by Bill
Basso. All rights reserved. Published by Grosset & Dunlap, a division of Penguin
Young Readers Group, 345 Hudson Street, New York, New York 10014. DRAGON
SLAYERS' ACADEMY and GROSSET & DUNLAP are trademarks of Penguin
Group (USA) Inc. Printed in the U.S.A.

Library of Congress Control Number: 2006100771

ISBN 978-0-448-44448-2                    10 9 8 7 6 5 4 3 2 1

# Chapter I

"**L**ook out, Angus!" yelled Wiglaf to his friend, who was perched atop a donkey.

Angus shouted, "Giddyap, Lumpen!"

But Lumpen didn't budge. And charging straight at Angus and Lumpen was an armor-clad lad riding a speedy black steed.

Wiglaf covered his eyes.

*CRASH!*

Wiglaf peeked through his fingers.

Angus lay in the dust looking surprised.

Wiglaf wasn't surprised. The Dragon Slayers' Academy jousting team had traveled to Knights' Noble Conservatory that morning by donkey cart. The KNC team was very good at jousting. The DSA team was very bad. The KNC team had real horses. The DSA team had a real donkey. Lumpen belonged to Frypot, the DSA cook. Wiglaf had washed a mountain of dishes to get Frypot to lend them Lumpen for the tournament.

Now they were in the KNC field behind the KNC castle. At either end of the field there were tents where students put on their armor—if they had any, which most of the DSA team did not. The fans sat on benches alongside the field.

"Oooh," groaned Angus, struggling to his feet. "You're supposed to run at the other team's steed, Lumpen."

Lumpen switched his tail.

"Worry not, Angus!" shouted Janice, the team captain, from the sidelines. She waved a DSA pennant and snapped her chewing gum. "You'll vanquish them next time!"

Janice had been a jousting champ at her old school. It had been her idea to start a DSA jousting team.

Now the KNC fans were cheering:

*"Rah, rah, rah for good old white and red!*
*Rah, rah, rah! We knocked you on your head!"*

Angus picked up his lance and limped over to Wiglaf, rubbing his backside.

"Want to switch, Wiggie?" he asked. "You joust, and I'll be team manager."

"No thanks," Wiglaf said. He liked his job. He cheered his team, brought snacks, arranged transportation to the jousting meets, and kept score.

The only thing Wiglaf didn't like was that his Class I not-so-little brother Dudwin had begged to be assistant team manager. At last Wiglaf gave in. Dudwin had traveled with Wiglaf and the team to KNC for the jousting match, where he was of no help whatsoever.

"Erica, you're up after Janice," Wiglaf said. "Time to armor up."

Erica hopped off the bench and stretched. "Zounds, but I have a good feeling about this!"

Erica was actually Princess Erica. She wanted to be a dragon slayer more than anything. She pumped a fist in the air and ran off to the tent to put on her armor.

"What's the score, Wiggie?" asked Dudwin.

"KNC has five hundred and eighty-two points," Wiglaf told him. "And we have—um—four points."

"We are such losers!" Dudwin moaned. "I wish DSA could win just once!"

Wiglaf wished so, too. But with Lumpen as their jousting steed, it wasn't likely.

"NEXT MATCH," boomed the announcer. "JANICE FROM DSA AGAINST LAUNCY FROM KNC."

Janice ran out and climbed on Lumpen's back. Lumpen bent his head and nibbled a tuft of grass.

At the far end of the field, Launcy from KNC mounted his steed. Launcy wore white armor with letters spelling out KNC. His white helmet sported a red plume. He held a long silvery lance.

"Fireball, charge!" cried Launcy, kicking his steed into a gallop. Down the field they ran, straight at Janice and Lumpen.

Janice gripped her lance. She chewed her gum faster and faster.

"Giddyap, Lumpen!" she shouted.

Lumpen did not move.

Wiglaf shut his eyes.

*CRASH!*

"Blazing King Ken's britches!" Angus yelled.

Wiglaf opened his eyes and gasped. "She stayed on!"

Dudwin started dancing and chanting:

*"Janice, Janice, she's our lass!*
*She's got spunk and she's got sass!*
*She's got heft and she's got mass!*
*Janice, Janice, she's first-class!"*

Janice blew a bubble and waved from her seat on top of Lumpen.

Launcy was sprawled on the ground, his white armor covered in dust.

The gong rang: *Bong! Bong!*

Halftime!

# Chapter 2

KNC cheerleaders dressed in red-and-white uniforms ran onto the jousting field, shouting:

*"Push DSA back, back, back into the woods,*
*'Cause they haven't, they haven't, they haven't got the goods!*
*And they haven't got the zazzle and they haven't got pizzazz,*
*And they haven't got the stuff that KNC has!"*

The KNC fans jumped up and cheered.

The DSA stands were empty except for Brother Dave, the DSA librarian. He had painted DSA in blue letters on his bald head. He waved a blue DSA flag.

"Goeth, DSA!" he yelled.

Erica, dressed in her armor, clanked out of the tent and over to her teammates.

Wiglaf passed around a flagon of Frypot's dragonmint eel ade.

Janice parked her gum behind her ear. She put the flagon to her lips, tossed back her head, and took a huge swig.

"Way to go, Janice!" said Angus. He slapped her on the back.

"Blaaaaahhh!" cried Janice as she spewed her mouthful of eel ade all over Wiglaf.

"Oops!" said Angus. "Sorry, Janice."

"Don't worry about it," said Janice, passing the flagon to Erica.

Cold, sticky eel ade ran down Wiglaf's face. It trickled down his neck. He eyed the stack of towels beside the KNC players' bench.

"Be right back," Wiglaf said. He jogged across the field with Dudwin following behind.

The KNC lads sat on their bench, wiping their

foreheads with red silk kerchiefs. Servants brought them rose-scented water and bathed their feet. They paid no attention to Wiglaf and Dudwin.

"Who wants to go dragon questing with me tomorrow in the Dark Forest?" Chauncy was saying. "I hear the hermit moved out of Hermit's Hovel and a dragon with a huge hoard of gold moved in."

Wiglaf had met a hermit once. His name was Crazy Looey, and the name fit. He wondered if Chauncy was talking about Looey's hovel.

"I hear it's a puny dragon," Chauncy went on. "Easy to slay."

"That's the kind I like!" Launcy said.

"I shall stab it with my lance!" said Flauncy.

"I shall slice off its head!" cried Delauncy. "There will be fountains of blood!"

Dudwin listened, fascinated.

But Wiglaf's stomach lurched. He hated hearing about bloody battles. He couldn't stand the sight of blood. And yet he was the only DSA student ever to slay a dragon. He had, in fact, killed two. But only by accident. He had done it by finding out the dragons' secret weaknesses. There had been no blood involved at all.

"Tell me more about this dragon," Launcy said.

Wiglaf did not want to hear any more about stabbing and jabbing and blood.

"Excuse me," Wiglaf said to the KNC lads. "May I borrow a towel?"

"A beautiful, clean KNC towel?" said Launcy. "For *you*?"

"Not a chance," said Chauncy. "Anyway, lads, as I was saying, this dragon is small and weak."

Wiglaf sighed. "Let's go, Dud."

"In a minute, Wiggie," Dudwin whispered.

Wiglaf jogged back to his teammates. But Dudwin stayed near the KNC lads, listening.

The jousting match ended. Wiglaf tallied up the final score:

**KNC:** *933*          **DSA:** *10*

"Art thou all present?" Brother Dave asked from the driver's seat as the DSA team climbed onto the donkey cart. "Then off we goest!"

He clicked his tongue. Lumpen began plodding back to DSA.

As the cart rolled over the drawbridge, Erica turned to look back at KNC.

"They sure have a beautiful castle." She sighed. "If DSA had all the fancy things KNC has, think how much we could learn! Maybe we'd even beat them at jousting."

"KNC lads go dragon hunting way more than we do," Dudwin said. "I heard them say they're going to slay a dragon tomorrow!"

"Class I will go a-slaying, Dud," Erica told him. "Be patient."

"Ha!" said Dudwin. "The KNC lads shall slay all the dragons. There won't be any left for us."

"No danger of that," said Angus. "Thousands of dragons live in the Dark Forest alone. New ones are hatching every day. Right, Wiggie?"

Wiglaf nodded. He thought back to the time when he and Angus had found a purple dragon's egg. They took it back to their dorm room, and it hatched. When the little dragon pipling first opened his eyes, he saw Wiglaf. So he called Wiglaf "Mommy." He called Angus "Sir." Wiglaf and Angus called him Worm. He was half-grown now and lived in the forest. But sometimes he flew back to DSA and stayed in the library, where Brother Dave kept him hidden from Headmaster Mordred. Wiglaf hadn't seen Worm in weeks. He hoped no harm had come to him.

"Let's sing that song we learned at Camp Dragononka!" Janice said. And she burst out singing:

*"One hundred flagons of mead on the wall,*
*One hundred flagons of mead!*
*If one of those flagons should happen to fall...*
*Ninety-nine flagons of mead on the wall."*

The rest of the team joined in.

Slimy eel ade trickled into Wiglaf's left ear. He sighed. It was going to be a long, sticky ride back to DSA.

# Chapter 3

Later that evening, Wiglaf ran down the steps to the Class I dorm to say good night to Dudwin. He peeked in at the door.

"The KNC lads are going dragon-questing," Dudwin was telling his friends.

"Lucky them!" said Bilge, Angus's cousin who was in Class I.

"Yeah, lucky them," said Maggot, Bilge's twin brother.

"I wish *we* could fight a dragon!" said a burly Class I lad.

"Me too," said Dudwin. "The KNC lads are going after a small dragon. It has a huge hoard of gold. Mountains of it!"

Dudwin did not see Wiglaf standing in the

doorway. He was having too much fun telling his story.

"It has pink ears," Dudwin continued. "So it's a boy dragon. And it has yellow eyes with cherry red centers."

Wiglaf gasped. Worm had yellow eyes with cherry red centers!

"They are going to slay this dragon tomorrow," Dudwin said.

*What if the KNC lads are after Worm!* thought Wiglaf. He didn't wait to hear any more. He raced back upstairs to the Class II dorm.

"Angus, wake up!" he cried, shaking his friend.

He told Angus what he had heard.

"This dragon sounds exactly like Worm!" Wiglaf said. "We must save him!"

Angus sat up. "You're right," he said. "But there are lots of KNC lads. Let's get Erica and Janice to help us."

"Good idea," said Wiglaf. "We can sneak over

to the lasses' dorm and tell them to pack up. We'll leave at dawn."

"What if Frypot catches us?" asked Angus. "He'll throw us in the dungeon for time-out, and we'll never save Worm."

Wiglaf frowned, thinking. At last he said, "I still have the Cap of Invisibility that Zelnoc gave Dudwin. If we stick very close together, I think it will turn both of us invisible."

Angus shook his head. "Zelnoc is the world's worst wizard. His spells always go wrong. If we put on that helmet, we could end up with five feet. Or nothing but arms!"

Wiglaf shrugged. "It's worth a try."

He reached under his cot and pulled out a bright blue cap covered with silver lightning bolts. He put it on his head, closed his eyes, and chanted: "Zippity zap!"

"Gadzooks!" cried Angus. "You vanished!"

Now Angus felt an invisible arm wrap around his shoulders. He looked down at where his feet should be. But he couldn't see them!

"Guess what? You're invisible, too!" said Wiglaf.

"'Tis true, I'm gone!" said invisible Angus. "But how do we walk like this?"

"We won the three-legged race on Field Day, remember?" said invisible Wiglaf. "Let's go."

The lads stumbled invisibly down the stone staircase and down the hall to the big wooden door. Wiglaf pushed it open. He peered into the castle yard. It looked empty.

"Egad!" whispered Angus. "What's *that?*"

Wiglaf saw it, too: a monstrous shape looming out of the dark. His heart nearly stopped.

"'Tis a dragon," he managed.

The dragon held very still. Wiglaf squinted into the night.

"Angus," he said, his heart beating once more. "'Tis only Old Blodgett, the practice dragon."

Angus sighed with relief.

The two crept invisibly across the castle yard. They tiptoed up the front steps of the Lasses' Dorm

Tower, nearly bumping into Frypot, who was standing guard at the foot of the tower.

"Who goes there?" squawked Frypot, sniffing suspiciously. "I smell eel."

*Uh-oh!* thought Wiglaf. *I still stink of eel ade! We're goners!* He crossed his fingers and held his breath.

"But then I always smell eel," Frypot muttered to himself. "That's what happens when you cook eels all day long. Eels, eels, eels. Never a nice swamp rat or a juicy pile of toads. What I could cook with some nice, plump leeches!"

Frypot stomped down the steps, still muttering.

Wiglaf watched him disappear into the dark. He let out his breath. Then the two lads slipped into the tower. They hurried invisibly up the winding stone staircase to the Class II Lasses' Dorm.

"Now to reappear," whispered Wiglaf. He let go of Angus.

Instantly, Angus became visible.

"Zappity zip!" Wiglaf chanted.

Nothing happened.

"Zappity zip!" Wiglaf said loudly.

Suddenly the door in front of them flew open. Erica stuck her head out.

"Angus?" she said. "What are you doing here?"

"I...uh," Angus sputtered as all the lasses jumped off their cots and ran to the doorway to see what was happening.

"Angus!" squealed Princess Gwendolyn of Gargglethorp. "Is this a raid?"

"No!" yelped Angus. "And it's not just me. Wiglaf is here, too."

"Where?" said Gwen. "I don't see him."

"Zappity zip!" shouted Wiglaf. Then he shouted, "OW!"

Angus and the lasses watched wide-eyed as Wiglaf's hands appeared, then disappeared. His nose appeared.

The lasses giggled.

"Yikes!" Wiglaf cried as his nose vanished and his left leg appeared. He reached up, grabbed the cap, and tugged with all his might. It popped off, and suddenly, all of Wiglaf was visible again.

Janice snapped her gum excitedly. "I love DSA!" she said. "There's always something crazy happening!"

"Shhhh!" warned Erica. "You don't want Frypot to catch them." She eyed Wiglaf. "So what are you doing here?"

"We need to talk to you and Janice," said Wiglaf.

The two lasses stepped out into the hallway. Wiglaf told them about the KNC lads and how Worm might be in danger.

"Lancelot's liver!" Janice said. "I remember Worm. He came to warn us about Snagglefahng."

"We must rescue him!" said Wiglaf.

"You're right, Wiggie," Erica said. "And we will. Normally we are dragon slayers—but now we shall be dragon savers!"

# Chapter 4

The next morning at dawn, Wiglaf and his friends knocked on the headmaster's door. It took some time before Mordred opened it. He glared at the four students with sleepy violet eyes.

"Wha...?" he said, clutching a teddy bear. "Oh, it's you, nephew."

"Good morning, Uncle Mordred," said Angus. "We must speak with you. It's an emergency."

"Emergency, schmemergency." Mordred stumbled back into bed. He pulled the covers up to his chin and closed his violet eyes. "You want me to spend my precious gold on fripperies like jousting uniforms and horses," he growled. "That isn't going to happen—ever. Now begone!"

Wiglaf stepped forward.

"Headmaster Mordred, sir," he said, "we

overheard the KNC lads talking yesterday. They say there's a small, weak dragon with a giant hoard of gold living in the Hermit's Hovel—"

Mordred's eyes flew open. "Giant hoard of gold?" he cried, sitting up. "Oh, Teddy," he cried, squashing his bear to his chest. "This could be the jackpot we've been dreaming of!" He seemed to notice the students again, and stuffed the teddy bear under his pillow.

"Well, what are you waiting for?" he barked. "Go and slay this dragon at once! Go, go, GO! Get me that GOLD!"

Wiglaf, Angus, Erica, and Janice scrambled out of the office. As they ran down the hall, Mordred stuck his head out the door.

"You'd better get to that dragon before the KNC lads do!" he bellowed.

"Yes, sir!" they yelled together.

The four hurried out into the castle yard. They had packed the night before. Wiglaf had his sword, Surekill. Erica had her sword and her Sir Lancelot tool belt. Janice was carrying her jousting lance. Angus was armed with a big bag of candy from his stash.

"I have a map of the Dark Forest from the Sir Lancelot Catalog," Erica said as they hurried toward the castle gate. "I shall lead the way."

As Wiglaf made way for Erica to take the lead he heard someone calling, "Wiglaf, wait!"

Wiglaf turned to see Dudwin running toward them.

"Where are you going, Wiggie?" Dudwin asked.

"On a dangerous quest," Wiglaf said. "You can't come."

Dudwin narrowed his eyes. "You're going dragon slaying, aren't you, Wiggie?"

"No, we're not," Wiglaf said truthfully. After all, they were going dragon *saving*, not dragon *slaying*.

"Yes, you are!" Dudwin cried. "And I'm coming!"

"No, Dud," said Wiglaf firmly. "You'll slow us down."

"I won't!" Dudwin protested.

"No," Erica said. "That is our final answer. Come on, team."

The Class II lads and lasses set off across the drawbridge. Wiglaf looked back. Dudwin was watching them go. His arms were crossed. He looked mad. Wiglaf felt bad, but there was no way his little brother could come. They had to travel fast to beat the KNC lads to Worm, or something terrible might happen!

"We need a name for our quest," Erica said as they walked up Huntsman's Path. She thought for a moment. "We should call ourselves WORM," she said at last. "The Worm Official Rescue Mission!"

Wiglaf grinned. "I like it."

"Me too," said Janice. "Hey, maybe that's what our jousting team needs—a cool name. What about the DSA Donkeys?"

Angus made a face.

WORM hurried along the road as the sun rose in the sky. At last they reached the Dark Forest. The trees were so thick that the sun barely peeked through. Even at midday it was dark.

And scary. Wiglaf heard strange calls from high in the trees. Strange hissing sounds came from the bushes. Strange growling sounds came from beside the path. But Wiglaf thought that might be Angus's stomach.

"I'm hungry," Angus said a moment later. "Let's stop for lunch."

"Wait!" said Erica. "Listen!"

They stopped. Wiglaf heard the usual Dark Forest noises. Then he heard a twig snap. He nearly jumped out of his boots.

Was something creeping up on them?

"Quick!" Erica whispered. "Over there!"

They ran to the mouth of a cave. It smelled bad. Worse than Frypot's leftover Eel Surprise. Worse than Bilge and Maggot's dead leech collection.

And it was very dark. But at least the cave seemed empty.

The four of them ran inside. They crouched down and listened.

*Step...step...step...*

Something was coming toward them through the bushes!

Wiglaf held his breath.

*CRACK!*

Another twig snapped.

Wiglaf shivered. And it wasn't from the cold.

A loud *THUMP!* sounded right outside the cave.

"AAAAAAAAAAAAAAAAAAAAAAAAH!" screamed the Worm Official Rescue Mission.

"AAAAAAAAAAAAAAAAAAAAAAAAH!" the something screamed right back at them.

Wiglaf peeked out through his fingers, expecting to see some wild creature.

What he saw was...

"Dudwin?" he cried. "What are you doing

here?" He stepped out of the cave. "And why were you screaming?"

"I screamed because you were." Then Wiglaf's little brother shrugged. "I'm coming on this quest with you, Wiggie." He folded his arms and stuck out his chin. "And there's nothing you can do to stop me."

Wiglaf knew that stubborn look. He'd seen it on all twelve of his brothers when their mother, Molwena, tried to stop their head-banging contests.

"I want to be the first Class I lad to slay a dragon," Dudwin added. "Like you were, Wiggie."

"Aw, let him come, Wiglaf," Angus said. "We need all the help we can get."

"Sure!" Janice said. "Dud's cool."

Erica stepped up to Wiglaf. "This way we can keep an eye on him," she said quietly. "Otherwise he might run ahead and get into trouble."

"All right, Dud," Wiglaf said. "You can come with us. But no picking up every rock you see."

"I won't," said Dudwin.

"And we are not going to slay this dragon," Wiglaf added.

"Sure we are!" Dudwin said. "We're dragon slayers!"

Wiglaf shook his head. "We think this dragon is our very own Worm, and we are going to rescue him from the KNC dragon slayers."

"Oh," said Dudwin. "That's not so exciting."

"You can go back to DSA," Wiglaf said eagerly.

"Nope," said Dudwin. "I'm coming. I want to see the dragon. And scare away KNC!"

Wiglaf sighed. "Fine."

But Dudwin didn't hear his brother. He was too busy climbing up the nearest tree.

# Chapter 5

ORM set off again, but now they moved more slowly. Dudwin kept climbing up trees to "scout ahead." He shouted down all that he saw from his perch and took his own sweet time climbing down.

"You never said no tree climbing," Dudwin said when Wiglaf complained.

"Keep up with us, Dud," said Wiglaf. "A young dragon's life may be at stake."

"All right, all right." Dudwin stomped ahead. "You sure know how to take all the fun out of a quest."

WORM sallied forth until the sun was high in the sky.

Angus stopped. "I can't go on without lunch,"

he declared. He sat down on a big rock and opened his stash bag.

"We must eat quickly," warned Wiglaf, "or we may be too late to save Worm!"

The others watched longingly as Angus gobbled up chocolate-covered boar jerky and taffy-apples while they nibbled on eel sandwiches that Erica had packed.

"Ah, that's better," said Angus, licking taffy from his fingers.

"Not for us," murmured Wiglaf.

Angus ignored him.

WORM took off again. They followed a trail that led farther into the forest.

They had not gone far when Angus said, "Are we almost there?"

Erica looked at her map. "Almost," she said.

But on and on they walked.

At last Wiglaf cried, "Look, a sign!"

It read:

HERMIT'S HOVEL THAT WAY ➡

An arrow pointed into the bushes.

Wiglaf scratched his head. "But there isn't a path that way."

"It's a trick," Erica said. "Hermits don't like to be bothered. So they put up signs telling people their hovels are in the opposite direction. My map of the Dark Forest says the hovel is this way."

On they went. Soon they came to another sign. It read:

IF YOU ARE TRYING TO REACH HERMIT'S HOVEL, YOU'RE ON THE WRONG PATH.

"That means we're on the right path," explained Erica.

A third sign was pinned to a tree. It read:

GOOD THING YOU'RE NOT LOOKING FOR A HERMIT.

BECAUSE YOU WON'T FIND ONE GOING THIS WAY.

"We must be close," said Janice.

The Worm Official Rescue Mission crept up the path until they came to a clearing. The trees had been cut down, letting in light. A small, broken-down hut sat in the middle of the clearing. Boards were nailed across its windows. The roof was full of holes.

There was a sign on the door: LOOEY DOESN'T LIVE HERE ANYMORE.

"Worm?" Wiglaf called. "Are you in there?"

But before he got an answer, lads in red-and-white KNC tunics ran toward the hovel from the opposite direction. They wore bright red feathers in their helmets and carried long, shiny swords. They surrounded the hovel.

Wiglaf counted them—ten, twelve, fourteen! His heart beat like a drum. How could the five of them take on fourteen well-armed KNC lads to save Worm?

"We know you're in there, dragon!" Launcy shouted in the direction of the hovel.

*"Ah-choo!"* came the reply.

*Is Worm sick?* Wiglaf wondered.

"We know you are small and weak!" shouted Chauncy.

"And easy to slay!" shouted Delauncy.

"Come out!" shouted Flauncy. "Or we're coming in!"

*"Dnoooo!"* came a voice from inside the hovel. *"Ggggggoooo wwayyyy! Ah-ah-ah-CHOOO!"*

Worm *was* in there! And he was definitely sick.

"Hold on, Worm!" yelled Wiglaf, darting out from behind the trees. "I'm coming!"

"Wiglaf, wait!" said Erica.

But it was too late. Wiglaf was speeding toward the hovel. His friends ran after him.

The KNC lads watched in surprise.

"Don't worry, Worm!" Wiglaf called. "We shall save you!"

"Back off, scruffy ruffians," shouted Chauncy. "Leave us to slay this beast."

From inside the hovel came a faint *"Bmommmmmmmy?"*

"Yes, Worm!" shouted Wiglaf. "It's me!"

Wiglaf heard sniffling and coughing and hacking inside the hovel. The dragon's nose was really stuffed up. He sounded awful!

"Begone, DSA!" said Flauncy, tossing his plume out of his eyes.

"But this is our dragon!" Angus said.

"We raised him from an egg," said Wiglaf. "We named him Worm."

"Oh, right!" Launcy said.

"You're trying to trick us to get the gold," said Chauncy.

"Worm has no gold," said Wiglaf.

"Back off, DSA," Chauncy snarled. "We're the best dragon slayers around, and we are going to prove it!"

Wiglaf heard a creaking noise. The door to the hovel was inching open. Worm's snout poked out. The dragon blinked his watery yellow-and-red eyes. His pink ears drooped. He coughed, and little puffs of smoke rose from his mouth.

"*Bmooommy?*" he bleated. "*Bmmoommmy! Wrrrrm hab cold.*"

"Did you hear the foul beast, lads?" Delauncy cried. "He has gold!"

"No!" Wiglaf shouted. "He doesn't have *gold*. He has a *cold*!"

Chauncy ignored him. "Prepare to slay!" he cried.

The KNC lads raised their swords and stepped forward.

Worm sniffled. "*Wrrrrm sssick.*"

"He says he's sick," said Delauncy, sounding worried.

"Aw, that's just some DSA trick," said Chauncy. "We charge on the count of three. One!"

Wiglaf had to do something—and fast.

"Stop!" Wiglaf cried. "Worm *is* sick. He has dragon pox!"

The KNC lads stopped. They lowered their swords.

Chauncy glared at Worm.

"Is it catching?" Angus said. "'Cause if it is, I'm—oof!"

Wiglaf elbowed his friend.

"That's right!" Erica said, getting what Wiglaf was doing. "Dragon pox is horrible. And very contagious to people!"

The KNC lads looked nervous.

"He has all the symptoms," Wiglaf said, looking at poor, droopy Worm. "Watery eyes, runny nose, flopping ears."

Worm closed his eyes and gave a giant "*AH-CHOOOO!*"

"Sneezing," said Wiglaf. "The pox come at the end."

Launcy, Flauncy, and several other KNC lads stepped back.

"*Doooon lettttt themmmm hrtttt bmmmeee!*" cried poor, stuffed-up Worm. He buried his face in Wiglaf's tunic.

Wiglaf waved Surekill at the KNC lads. He tried to look threatening.

"Begone!" he shouted. "Begone before you fall sick with the dread dragon pox!" Wiglaf tried to sound commanding, and maybe he was, because suddenly all the KNC lads froze. Their eyes opened wide.

"AAAAAAAAAAAH!" screamed Chauncy.

"AAAAAAAAAAAAAH!" screamed Launcy.

"AAAAAAAAAAAAAAAAAAAAAAAAAH!!!" screamed Flauncy and Delauncy and all the rest of the KNC lads.

The whole pack turned and ran helter-skelter into the forest. They ran as if there were a herd of fire-breathing dragons after them.

Wiglaf smiled. He had no idea he could scare anyone so much.

Then suddenly Angus was screaming, too: "AAAAAAAAAAAAAAAAAAAH!"

"AAAAAAAAAAAAAAAAAAAAAAAAH!"

screamed Dudwin.

Even Erica let out a yelp.

Janice stopped chewing gum and stared. Then they all turned and ran away from the hovel.

*What is going on?* Wiglaf wondered. *How can they be scared of me?*

All at once Wiglaf felt the ground shake. A large shadow appeared in front of him. Slowly he turned to see what was making the shadow. He looked up.

And up.

And up.

Looming over the hovel was a little lass of four or five years old.

Only she wasn't little.

She was a giant!

# Chapter 6

"**O**H, WOOK!" boomed the giant lass as she thundered a few steps to the hovel door. "A WIDDLE DWAGON!"

Her hand came down, down, down from the sky. A grubby finger flicked Wiglaf out of the way.

"Yaaaaah!" he cried as he flew, landing on a nearby bush.

The giant lass plucked Worm up and lifted him into the sky.

"A PWETTY DWAGON!" she cried. "I AWWAYS WANTED A WEAL WIVE DWAGON!"

"*Bmmmmmmmmmooooommmmmmmmy!*" Worm squealed.

"Stop, giant!" Wiglaf yelled, scrambling to his feet. "Put that dragon down!"

The giant lass looked all around. "WHO'S SQUEAKING?" she boomed.

"ME!" Wiglaf yelled at her. "Don't take that dragon!"

Now the giant lass bent down and peered at Wiglaf. Her giant face came closer and closer. His heart beat fast with fear. She could squash him with her giant thumb if she wanted to.

The giant lass wrinkled her nose. "AWE YOU A BUG?" she asked.

"No," Wiglaf said. "That dragon is my friend. Please don't take him."

"BUT I *WANTS* IT," the giant lass explained. "AND GIANTS AWWAYS TAKES EVEWYTHING THEY WANTS."

"But that's stealing!" Wiglaf cried.

"GIANTS WOVE TO STEAW!" said the giant lass.

"It's not right," said Wiglaf. "The dragon doesn't

belong to you."

"DOES NOW!" the giant lass hollered back. "IT'S *MY* DWAGON! HOOWAY!"

"No!" shouted Wiglaf. "Put him down!"

"MINE, MINE, MIIIIIIIIINE!" she shouted, stamping her feet. The ground shook, knocking Wiglaf over.

"WET'S GO TO MY CASTLE, DWAGON," bellowed the giant lass. "YOU CAN BE BESTEST FWIENDS WITH MY STUFFED PINKY DWAGON. I GONNA DWESS YOU UP WIKE A PWINCESS AND MAKE YOU SOOO PWETTY!"

"Oh, woe is Worm!" murmured Wiglaf.

"I GONNA KEEP YOU IN A CAGE, DWAGON," the giant lass went on. "I GONNA GIVE YOU A BATH AND FEED YOU WOWWIPOPS."

The giant lass dropped Worm into her sparkly pink purse and snapped it shut. Then she stomped off into the Dark Forest.

"Wait!" Wiglaf cried. He ran after her as fast as he could. But soon she was so far ahead that he could not see her anymore.

Wiglaf stopped. He looked around. He had lost Worm. He had lost his friends. And now he was lost and alone in the Dark Forest. So much for the Worm Official Rescue Mission.

Wiglaf needed help. There was only one thing to do.

"Conlez, Conlez, Conlez!" he chanted, summoning the wizard Zelnoc by saying his name backward three times.

POOF!

A white flash lit up the forest. When it vanished, there stood Zelnoc. The wizard was holding a knife and fork. His long white beard was hooked over one ear. A bib was tucked into the neck of his robe.

"Bats and blisters!" the wizard cried. "I was just sitting down to a plate of roasted newts. Powerful food, newts. All sorts of spell-enhancing vitamins and mincrals. Who blew out all the torches?"

"You're in the Dark Forest, Zelnoc," Wiglaf said.

"Woglott?" Zelnoc said, squinting. "You again?"

"I need your help," Wiglaf said.

"What else is new?" Zelnoc grumbled. He slipped his knife and fork into his robe pocket. "Tell me what you want, and make it snappy. Newts lose their zing if they sit around."

"A giant stole Worm," Wiglaf said.

Zelnoc frowned. "What does a giant want with a worm?"

"Worm is the name of the baby dragon Angus and I raised," Wiglaf said. "Remember?"

"So a giant stole a dragon," said Zelnoc. "And you want me to...what?"

"Help me find him," said Wiglaf. "He's only a little dragon, and he's sick. And I need to find my friends, too."

The wizard's eyes lit up.

"I have just the thing!" he exclaimed. He

reached under his hat and pulled out a long, fluffy yellow feather. "Ta-da!"

Wiglaf was confused. "What is that?"

"This is my very own invention." Zelnoc waved the feather. "Eat your heart out, Zizmor!"

"Will the feather help me find Worm?" Wiglaf asked.

"Not...exactly," said Zelnoc.

"Will it help me find my friends?" asked Wiglaf.

"Well...no," said Zelnoc.

"Will it help me vanquish the giant?" Wiglaf asked.

"Doubtful," said Zelnoc.

Wiglaf sighed. This sounded like another one of Zelnoc's featherbrained ideas.

"Then what can the feather do?" Wiglaf asked.

"Not a feather," said Zelnoc, sounding insulted. "It's a quill. A Quickening Quill. It can bring any object to life!"

"Really?" said Wiglaf. He was afraid to think

about how many ways a spell like that might go wrong.

"Just watch," Zelnoc said. He marched up to the nearest boulder and began tickling it with the feather. As he tickled, he chanted:

*"Tickle, tickle, how time flies,*
*I'm waking you up, so now ARISE!"*

Zelnoc stepped back.

A crack appeared across the front of the boulder. Then the crack opened. It was a mouth! And the rock began to speak.

"URGH!" said the rock.

"See? It worked!" Zelnoc cried in delight.

"URGH!" said the rock. Slowly, slowly, it began to roll.

"Wait," said Zelnoc. "Stop right there, rock."

"URGH! URGH!" said the boulder. It started rolling faster. And faster. It rolled off down the hill, picking up speed as it went.

"Look at that rock go!" shouted Zelnoc. "What a quill!" He kissed his feather. "I'd better go reverse the spell. Zizmor doesn't like to have inanimate objects running around. I used the quill on his wizard shoes once. By the time we caught up to them, they were starring in a tap-dancing show in East Ratswhiskers."

He thrust the quill into Wiglaf's hand. "Good luck, Waglurp!"

"Wait!" Wiglaf cried. "How do I turn off the spell?"

"Just chant *Gootchie, gootchie, ham and pickle!*" Zelnoc yelled as he ran after the rock. *"Be as you were before..."* The wizard's voice trailed off in the distance.

"Before *what?*" Wiglaf called after him.

Zelnoc was speeding after the rock and didn't hear him.

Wiglaf looked at the fluffy yellow feather in his hand.

Now what was he supposed to do?

# Chapter 7

Wiglaf wondered what in the Dark Forest he might bring to life that would help him find his friends, the giant's castle, and Worm.

Maybe if he woke up a tall tree, it would be able to see his friends and tell him where they were.

Wiglaf walked around until he found a very tall tree. He took the feather and started tickling under the tree's branches.

*"Tickle, tickle, how time flies,"* Wiglaf began.

"Stooooop it!" said a deep voice.

Wiglaf spun around. There was no one behind him.

"Whaaaat in the naaaame of King Aaaarthur aaare you doooing?" said the voice.

"I—I—" Wiglaf stammered. "I'm trying to bring this tree to life."

Leaves rustled above him. "Isn't thaaat just like a humaaaaan," the tree said. "I'm aaaalready aliiiive."

"You can talk!" Wiglaf said. "Can all trees talk?"

"Whyyy don't you tiiickle aaaall of theeem and fiiiind ooout?" the tree said. "Aaand theeen *I* caaaan gooo baaaack to sleeeeeep."

"Wait!" Wiglaf said. "Can you please help me find my friends?"

Leaves rustled again. "Dooo your frieeeends incluuuude a biiig laaaass with a laaaaance? A stout laaaaad? A laaaass who aaaacts like she knooows everythiiing? And a laaaad who's fooond of cliiiimbing treeees?"

"That's them!" Wiglaf said excitedly. "Where are they?"

"Sorry. Haven't seen 'em," said the tree. Its branches quivered, and Wiglaf had the feeling it was laughing.

"Please tell me where they are," Wiglaf pleaded.

"Aaaaall riiiight," said the tree. "If yoooou wiiiill leeeeaf me aloooone. Geeet it? *Leeeeaf* me aloooone?"

"I get it," said Wiglaf. "Now where are my friends?"

"Gooo foooorty braaaanch lengths thaaaat waaaay." The tree pointed a branch to the north.

"Thank you, tree," said Wiglaf. "Nice talking to you. Farewell!"

Wiglaf tucked the feather into his belt and headed north. He went slowly through the dark, feeling his way. He had not gone far when he spied a dim light ahead of him. He heard voices.

"We must find Wiglaf!" Erica was saying.

"I thought he was running right behind me," Angus said.

"Giants cat peuple," Janice said.

"I hope Wiglaf didn't get eaten!" said Dudwin.

"I didn't," said Wiglaf, stepping out from behind a tree into a circle of light from a campfire.

Dudwin leaped up and ran to his brother. He threw his arms around him. "Why do you have a big yellow feather stuck in your belt, Wiggie?" he asked.

"Zelnoc gave it to me," Wiglaf said. "Something terrible has happened," he added. "The giant picked up Worm and took him back to her castle."

"She dragon-napped him?" asked Angus.

Wiglaf nodded. "The giant lass is going to bathe Worm and dress him up in fancy princess clothes and feed him lollipops and keep him in a cage."

"A cage?" cried Janice. "That's terrible!"

"Fancy clothes?" said Erica. "That's horrible!"

"A bath?" cried Dudwin. "That's the WORST!"

"The lollipops don't sound so bad," offered Angus.

"We have to find Worm," said Wiglaf. He frowned. "But I don't know which way the giant went."

"That's easy," said Erica. "She's a giant, so all we have to do is look for giant footprints...and follow them."

Erica unhooked the mini-torch from her tool belt. She lit it, and WORM began walking in the direction of the Hermit's Hovel.

"I think she went this way," said Wiglaf.

Erica, Janice, and Angus followed Wiglaf. Dudwin ran off in the opposite direction.

"Dud, come back!" called Wiglaf.

"Be right there, Wiggie!" Dudwin answered. "I want to climb up a tall tree over...OOPS!"

Wiglaf heard the sound of his not-so-little brother hitting the ground. He and the others ran toward him.

"Dud?" he called. "Where are you?"

"Down here!" Dudwin answered.

Wiglaf and the others looked around.

"Here he is!" said Janice. "He fell in a shallow ditch." She held out a hand and pulled Dudwin out.

Erica stepped closer and held her mini-torch over the ditch.

"That's no ditch," she said. "That's the giant lass's footprint!"

"Good job, Dudwin!" said Janice.

Dudwin grinned.

"There's the next footprint!" said Wiglaf, pointing. "And the next!"

"Come on," Erica said. "We shall follow them to the giant lass's castle."

She pointed her mini-torch toward the ground. The flame made a circle of light just big enough for them to see the footprints.

"I shall be the lookout!" Dudwin yelled, running ahead and scrambling up a tree.

"We don't need a lookout, Dud!" Wiglaf called. "We're following footprints."

But Dudwin was already halfway up the trunk.

He came down at last, and the Worm Official Rescue Mission walked on.

After a while, Wiglaf became aware that it was growing light. He glanced up.

"The sun's up," said Wiglaf. "We're not in the Dark Forest anymore."

"That's good," said Angus. "That forest gives me the creeps. I don't like it when it's so dark and..." He stopped, looking around. "Whoa, where are we?"

They were standing on a wide dirt path. A path ten times wider than any Wiglaf had ever seen before.

"Why would a path need to be this wide?" asked Janice.

"And what's with these hedges?" asked Erica. "They're taller than the hedges at the Royal Palace."

"Wait a minute," said Wiglaf. "It's not a hedge. It's grass!"

"Grass doesn't grow this tall," said Angus.

"This grass does," Janice said.

Wiglaf shivered. A path wide enough for ten wagons side by side. Grass taller than he was. Where *were* they?

"There's a sign up ahead," said Dudwin.

The five stuck very close together as they approached a big sign at the top of a tall pole.

"What's it say, Wiggie?" asked Dudwin.

Wiglaf leaned his head way back and looked up, up, up. It took him a while, but at last he made out the letters spelling out a message.

"It says '*You Must Be This Tall to Enter Gigantia*,'" read Wiglaf.

"So this is the Kingdom of Gigantia," said Erica. "I've heard of it, but I never knew where it was."

"A kingdom of giants!" Janice exclaimed. She blew a giant bubble. "This is so cool! Let us be off!"

"We can't!" said Angus. "We're too short to enter. We have to go back."

"We are on a mission!" said Erica. "Nothing shall stop us from saving Worm. Especially not some stupid sign."

Wiglaf smiled. Erica was the bravest person he knew.

# Chapter 8

There were more giant footprints on the wide dirt path. "The giant lass must have come this way," said Erica. "Follow me! Forward, march!"

Erica led the way along the side of the path. The others followed her.

"If someone comes along, we can duck into the grass and hide," Erica said as they marched.

"I hope Worm appreciates what we're doing for him," Angus muttered.

After a while, WORM came to another sign.

This time Janice read it:

"WELCOME TO GIGANTIA, LAND OF GIANTS.

GIANTS ONLY! THIS MEANS YOU!

TRESPASSERS WILL END UP IN THE
STEW."

"We're really in the Land of Giants!" said
Dudwin. "Wait'll I tell the other Class I kids!"

Wiglaf only hoped Dudwin might live to tell
about being here. He felt his knees shaking. He did
not want to end up in a stew. But Worm needed
their help. They had to go on.

"Fighting giants is better than slaying dragons,"
Dudwin said. "Giants have treasure, too, don't they?
Maybe we can get some gold."

"You sound like my uncle Mordred," said
Angus.

They came to the foot of a hill.

"This hill is going to require some caramel
candy," said Angus, opening his stash bag again.

"I could use a caramel," said Wiglaf.

"Me too," said Dudwin.

"We all could," said Erica.

"How about sharing today, Angus?" said Janice.

Angus sighed loudly. "Just this once," he said. "Then it's back to my basic No-Sharing Policy." He handed each of his friends a single caramel, and they started up the hill.

Erica was first to reach the top.

"Look!" she said. "Over there! A castle!"

Wiglaf saw it, too. It stood on the top of a steep, rocky hill.

"We're not climbing *that*, are we?" Angus asked. "How do we even know that's the right castle?"

"You see any others?" asked Erica. "And it's big—giant-size, in fact."

"We're doing this for Worm, Angus," said Wiglaf. "He needs our help!"

Angus sighed. "This is going to require marshmallows." He sat down, pulled out his stash of Medieval Marshmallows, and ate them all. He did not offer to share, so the others made do with the remains of their eel sandwiches.

The sun was setting as the Worm Official Rescue Mission started up the steep, rocky hill. Dudwin scrambled up in no time. Angus kept slipping on the stones. Once, he nearly rolled back down.

At last they reached the giant's castle. It was an old castle with crumbling stones covered in moss and vines. The moat was empty. The castle wall was a jumble of rocks.

Keeping low, the five made their way toward the castle.

Wiglaf heard rumbling. He turned to see a giant wooden cart illuminated by two flaming torches clattering up the hill. It was pulled by a giant donkey, fifty times the size of Lumpen. A giant woman with blond curls sat in the back. The driver was a surly-looking goblin half her size, with swamp green skin, bushy hair, and crooked yellow teeth.

"Hide!" Erica whispered. They all scurried behind a craggy rock and peeked out.

The cart pulled up to the door and stopped.

"GRIT!" The giant shouted so loudly that Wiglaf felt the rock tremble. "THE DOOR!"

The door creaked open.

"This is our chance!" whispered Erica. "Quick, jump onto the back of the cart!"

Wiglaf's heart thumped as they scrambled across the rocks to the cart. Dudwin quickly climbed up the wheel spokes. He helped pull the others up after him. They huddled together on the back of the cart.

Wiglaf's teeth rattled as the cart wheels thundered over the rocks and through the giant doorway. The cart stopped inside what looked like a stable. The giant swung down from the cart.

Another surly-looking goblin scurried toward the cart. He wore a dirty white jacket.

"So good to have you home, Lady Whopping-Large," the goblin said in a wheedling voice.

"UNHARNESS CLIP-CLOP, GRIT," the giant ordered the goblin. "I'VE BEEN DRIVING FOR HOURS. I HOPE YOU'VE COOKED ME A GOOD SUPPER. I'M SO HUNGRY, I COULD EAT A HORSE."

"HEE-HAW!" said Clip-Clop nervously.

"Indeed, Lady Whopping-Large," said the goblin, grinning and bowing as he unharnessed the donkey. "I made you a lovely blood pudding."

Blood pudding? Wiglaf felt his stomach lurch.

"MUMMY!" screamed a high-pitched voice. Wiglaf peered around the side of the cart and saw the giant lass running toward her mother. She threw her arms around her in a giant hug.

"GUESS WHAT!" the giant lass squealed. "I FOUND A WEAL DWAGON FOR ME TO PWAY WITH!"

"YOU CAN TELL ME ALL ABOUT IT WHILE WE EAT SUPPER, GRUBELLA," said the mother giant.

The mother and daughter giants headed up a stone staircase.

"I PUT THE WEAL DWAGON IN A CAGE IN MY WOOM," bellowed Grubella as they went. "I DWESSED HER UP WITH

A PWINCESS HAT WITH PINK WIBBONS. SHE CAN BE FWIENDS WITH MY STUFFED PINKY DWAGON."

Wiglaf's heart sank. Pink ribbons! Poor Worm.

"I GONNA HAVE TEA WIF MY DWAGONS AND MY DOWWIES," Grubella went on. "AND I GONNA CAWW MY WEAL DWAGON PWINCESS SPAWKLE."

"PRINCESS SPARKLE!" exclaimed the mother giant. "WHAT A PWETTY—I MEAN, PRETTY NAME FOR YOUR DRAGON."

The giants disappeared into the castle. Wiglaf heard no more.

"Princess Sparkle, indeed!" huffed Erica.

WORM waited until Grit led Clip-Clop off to his stall. Then Wiglaf and his friends jumped off the back of the wagon. They hurried over to the stone steps. Each one was twice as tall as Wiglaf.

"How are we going to get into the castle?" he asked. "We're too small to climb up those steps."

"I can climb them," said Dudwin. "I can climb anything."

"Here," said Erica, taking a coil of rope from her tool belt and handing it to Dudwin. "When you get to the top, throw it down to us."

Dudwin managed to find toeholds in the stone and soon climbed up the five steps. He threw the rope down and held it as, one by one, the others climbed up. It took a long time for them all to get to the top of the stairs.

"I'm so hungry!" Angus whimpered.

"Too bad," said Erica. "We are on a mission. We must find Grubella's room. Follow me."

She led the way down a long torch-lit hallway, keeping close to the wall. Wiglaf felt no bigger than a mouse. There were giant-size doors all along the hallway.

Through a door to his left, Wiglaf saw a vast dining hall. Inside stood a table as long as a jousting field, with tall wooden chairs around it. But the table and chairs were covered with dust.

Faded, moth-eaten tapestries hung on the walls. Wiglaf got the feeling that the Whopping-Large castle had seen better days.

On they went, down the long hallway. From the doorway to the kitchen, Wiglaf saw flames flickering and leaping inside a giant oven. A giant basket had tipped over, spilling giant apples onto the floor. Grit was stomping about, banging pots and pans and grumbling to himself about Lady Whopping-Large.

"Cheap, that's what she is," the goblin muttered. "Can't make a decent supper on twopence a day. If only I could find a steady source of humans." He licked his deep green lips with a pointy pink tongue and sighed. "That would spice up my stew."

Angus shuddered. "Do giants really eat humans?" he whispered.

"Only if they catch us," Janice whispered back.

"Which they won't!" Erica added quickly.

Suddenly a huge *THUMP!* sounded behind them.

Then another.

*THUMP!*

*THUMP!*

Footsteps!

Wiglaf turned just in time to see Lady Whopping-Large clomping down the hall—straight toward them!

# Chapter 9

"**Q**uick!" yelped Wiglaf. "Hide!"

The five tumbled into the kitchen. They ran pell-mell across the floor and dove into the tipped-over basket of giant apples.

Wiglaf crouched behind an apple and held his breath.

Lady Whopping-Large stomped into the kitchen. She stopped and sniffed the air.

*Oh, no!* Wiglaf thought. *Can she smell us?* If she could smell humans, she'd probably smell Dudwin. He'd never taken a bath in his life.

"FEE FIE FO FUM!" the giant boomed. "I SMELL STEW MADE OF LEECH POND SCUM!"

*Whew!* Wiglaf thought. *It's only the stew.*

"IS THIS STEW FOR DINNER TOMORROW WHEN LORD WHOPPING-LARGE GETS HOME?" asked the giant.

Her voice was so loud that Wiglaf bounced around in the apples.

"'Tis, Lady Whopping-Large." The goblin grinned and bowed. "Tastes better than it smells. Nicely spiced, if I do say so myself."

"FUM FEE FO FIE," grumbled the giant. "ALL I WANT IS A HUMAN PIE."

Wiglaf started trembling. And then he heard a...

*Crunch!*

He froze. What was that?

"YOU HEAR THAT, GRIT?" asked the giant.

Grit nodded. "Must be mice in the pantry," he said.

*Crunch!*

Wiglaf turned toward the sound, and his heart nearly stopped. Angus was taking bites out of a giant apple!

Wiglaf motioned to him to cut it out! But Angus pretended not to notice.

*Crunch!*

"SET SOME TRAPS, GRIT," said the giant. She stomped out of the kitchen.

Wiglaf went limp with relief. What was Angus thinking?

"Come on," Erica whispered. "The goblin is busy with the stew. Now's our chance!"

They slipped out of the basket and scurried across the kitchen floor. They ran through the doorway to the hallway and stopped to catch their breath.

"You almost landed us in the stew, Angus!" said Erica.

"I couldn't help it," said Angus. "I was *so* hungry."

Quick as mice, the five scampered down the torch-lit hallway until they came to a stone spiral staircase. A worn red carpet lay on the floor at the bottom of the stairs. Big pieces of parchment painted with crude drawings were stuck to the walls all the way up the stairs. The drawings showed dragons wearing frilly outfits. Dragons having tea. Dragons painting their toenails. Wiglaf shook his head. This would be Worm's fate if they didn't save him!

"This staircase must lead to Grubella's room," said Erica.

"It took us forever to climb the five steps from the stable," Wiglaf said. "It'll take us all night to climb these!"

"I wish we had a flying carpet," Dudwin said.

"That would be so cool!" said Janice.

"Maybe we will," said Wiglaf, staring at the frayed red carpet.

"What are you talking about, Wiggie?" asked Erica.

"This." Wiglaf pulled the Quickening Quill from his belt. He quickly explained how the wizard had given him the feather and what it was supposed to do. "I might be able to turn this into a flying carpet," he said.

"I don't know," said Erica. "That wizard's spells have a way of going wrong."

"I say we try it," Janice said. "What's the worst that could happen?"

"Oh, the spell could stop working in midair," Angus said, "and we fall to our deaths. Or the rug might throw us off, and *then* we fall to our deaths. Or—"

"Enough, Angus," Erica said. "We have no choice." She turned to Wiglaf. "Go on. Try it."

Wiglaf began tickling the carpet with the feather and chanting:

*"Tickle, tickle, how time flies,*
*I'm waking you up, so now ARISE!"*

The edges of the carpet began to flap.

"Oh my!" said a bubbly voice. The carpet flapped harder, and the whole thing rose up until it floated above the stone floor. Then the carpet gave itself a good shake. Dust filled the air.

Wiglaf and his friends backed away until the dust storm ended.

"Oh, I feel *so* much better!" exclaimed the carpet.

"Excuse me, carpet," Wiglaf said as the dust settled. "We need your help. Could you please fly us to the top of these stairs?"

"Are you jesting?" The carpet folded itself, as if arching its back, and rose higher into the air. "I'm finally free to move about on my own, and what happens? Someone wants a lift! Well! I've let people walk all over me my whole life and this is where it ends. I have to stand up for myself! I have to do what's right for *me* for once!" The rug gave a forceful flounce.

"We don't mean to order you around, carpet," Erica said. "We just need to get up the stairs."

"Please help us," said Angus.

"You wouldn't even be floating around if my brother hadn't put a spell on you," Dudwin pointed out.

"I said no, and I meant no," the carpet said. "I'm going on a holiday. Ta-ta!" It began to float toward a slit in the castle wall.

Erica rushed toward the fleeing carpet. She drew her sword. "Don't make me use this, rug!" she called.

The carpet sighed. "Oh, have it your way," it said, floating down and hovering inches above the floor. "Jump on."

The five stepped onto the carpet, knelt down, and grabbed hold of the edges. They held tight as the carpet began spiraling up the stairs, gaining speed with every turn.

"Wheeee!" shouted the carpet. "I never knew what I was missing just lying around on the floor!"

"This is so cool!" said Janice.

"Amazing!" said Dudwin. "Wait'll I tell the other Class I kids!"

Wiglaf gripped the edges of the carpet. He did

not look down. He tried not to think about what would happen if the spell stopped working and they fell. He kept his thoughts on saving Worm.

The rug rounded a final bend, hovered for a moment, then floated down onto the landing at the top of the stairs.

"Second floor," the carpet said. "Everybody off!"

Wiglaf and the others hopped off.

"Thanks, carpet," Dudwin said. "That was awesome!"

Wiglaf pulled the Quickening Quill from his belt. He knew he should reverse the spell. Zizmor would not be happy to have a carpet floating around the world. But what was that spell-reversing rhyme anyway? Something about ham and pickles, be as you were before...what? Oh, well. It seemed too cruel to turn the flying carpet into a mere rug again.

"Have a good holiday, carpet!" he called as the carpet floated up again.

"I shall!" the carpet answered. "I'm outta here!" Then it rolled itself up and shot through the narrow slit in the castle wall.

"Now to rescue Worm," Wiglaf said.

But before anyone could take a step, a giant roar filled the air.

# Chapter 10

he roar sounded again.

"What's *that*?" whispered Wiglaf.

"Sounds like Pa, snoring," said Dudwin.

Wiglaf smiled. That's exactly what it sounded like! The giant lass was snoring.

"Guess we follow the snoring," said Erica.

The roaring grew louder as she led the way down a hallway to a tower room. Moonlight shone through slits in the castle wall. A small torch flickered by the doorway. Everything was lit by the glow. Grubella lay sleeping in a giant bed, holding a pink, plush dragon. Her mouth was wide open, and she was indeed snoring: *HONNNN-BUBUBUBUBUBUBUBRRRRRR!*

"She's awfully loud!" shouted Dudwin over

the giant lass's snoring.

"Shhhhhhhhhhhhhhh!" Wiglaf said frantically.

Grubella snorted and rolled over in her sleep. She stuck her giant thumb into her giant mouth. At least she wasn't snoring anymore.

Wiglaf looked around the room. Where was Worm? He spied a giant birdcage sitting on a low table next to Grubella's bed. And curled up on the bottom of the cage was Worm. He had a lacy pink princess hat tied onto his head. His claws had been painted with sparkly pink polish. His tail drooped through the bars of the cage. His snout was running.

"He still looks sick," Wiglaf whispered. "He needs Brother Dave's Heavenly Cold-B-Gone Tonic." He turned to Janice. "Boost me up onto the table. I'll open the door to his cage."

Janice knitted her fingers together and lowered her hands. Wiglaf stepped onto them. Slowly, Janice raised her arms. Wiglaf reached up and grabbed onto the edge of the table with

his fingertips. He dangled for a moment. Then he kicked one leg up onto the table and pulled the rest of himself up, too.

"Way to go, Wiggie!" said Dudwin.

"Shhhhhhh, Dud!" warned Erica.

"PWETTY," murmured Grubella. But she did not open her eyes.

Wiglaf tiptoed across the bedside table to the cage. He climbed up the bars until he reached the cage door. He pulled.

The door stayed shut.

Wiglaf slid down the cage bars and ran to the edge of the table. "Locked!" he mouthed.

"We must find the key," Erica mouthed back.

The other dragon rescuers searched everywhere on the floor—under Grubella's giant bed, under her giant chest of drawers, under her giant toy chest.

No key.

Wiglaf searched everywhere on top of the table. He peered under Grubella's dolls. Under a stuffed boar and basilisk. Under a tiny stuffed unicorn.

No key.

Now Worm raised his head from the bottom of the birdcage. *"Mommmy?"* he burbled. *"Mmmommmmmy! Wrrrm happy see you!"*

"Shhhh!" Wiglaf placed a finger to his lips. "I'm happy to see you, too, Worm," he whispered. "We shall find the key to your cage and rescue you. Don't make any noise, okay?"

*"Tank you, Mommmmmy!"* Worm said softly. Then he sneezed—loudly. *"AHHH-CHOOO!"*

Grubella's eyelids fluttered, but her eyes stayed closed.

"Wiggie, catch!" Dudwin half whispered.

The next thing Wiglaf knew, he was holding tight to one end of a rope. His brother was holding the other, climbing up the table leg.

Dudwin reached the top of the table and hurried over to Worm's cage.

"Egad! A real, live dragon!" he exclaimed. "Wait'll I tell the other Class I kids about *this!*"

Then Dudwin crawled nearer to Grubella. "Hey, Wiggie! The giant's doll has on a gold bracelet. Look—it's got a gold crown charm. You think it's real gold?"

"Who knows?" said Wiglaf. He picked up the skirt of a troll doll and peered under it. "We're looking for the key, remember?"

"The key isn't down here!" Janice called from the floor. "Pull us up, Dud. We need to make a plan."

Dudwin let down the rope, and Erica, Janice, and Angus climbed up. Angus patted Worm through the bars of the cage.

"*Sirrrr,*" trilled Worm.

"Planning time," said Erica, hooking her rope back onto her tool belt. "Everybody think hard about how we can save Worm."

"*Tink harrrrrd!*" Worm said.

Wiglaf thought hard. At last he said, "Grubella opens and closes the cage door. So she obviously knows where the key is."

"Well, we can't exactly ask her where it is," said Erica.

"Why not?" he said, and he jumped lightly from the table onto the giant lass's bed.

"What are you doing, Wiggie?" called Dudwin.

Wiglaf didn't answer. He froze while Grubella rolled over in her sleep. Then he slogged across her pillows until he was right beside her giant ear.

"Grubella...Grubella..." Wiglaf whispered. "Where is the key to the dragon's cage? Where is the key?"

Grubella snorted and rolled over, nearly squashing Wiglaf.

"Grubella!" Wiglaf tried again. "Tell me where the key is."

"THE KEY," Grubella mumbled in her sleep. "I GOTS THE KEY."

All of a sudden Wiglaf heard the *THUMP THUMP* of giant footsteps.

"*Hiiiiiddde, Mmoommmmmy!*" burbled Worm.

Everyone hid. Wiglaf dove under Grubella's plush Pinky Dragon.

*THUMP THUMP!*

Someone was coming up the stairs!

# Chapter II

"**Y**OU LOOK SO SWEET WHEN YOU'RE ASLEEP, GRUBELLA," said the giant mom as she tiptoed over to her daughter's bed. She leaned over and kissed Grubella's forehead. Then she patted the stuffed pink dragon.

Underneath the dragon, Wiglaf jiggled up and down and wondered—was he about to be squished?

Now Wiglaf heard Lady Whopping-Large sniffing.

"FIE FEE FOO FING," she said. "THIS ROOM REEKS OF HUMAN BEING." She smacked her lips. "THEY SMELL SO BAD, BUT THEY TASTE SOOOO GOOD. OH, WHAT I WOULDN'T DO FOR A HUMAN SNACK RIGHT NOW!"

*Egad!* Wiglaf thought. *She's going to find us and eat us!*

Wiglaf heard the giant take a few steps. Then he heard more sniffing.

"AH! SO IT'S *YOU* THAT SMELLS LIKE HUMANS, DRAGON," she said.

"*Mmmmmeee?*" Worm trilled.

Wiglaf heard more sniffing.

"YOU," the giant said. "TOMORROW, PRINCESS SPARKLE, YOU ARE GETTING A BATH."

Wiglaf heard the giant tiptoe out of Grubella's room. He breathed a huge sigh of relief. Then he stuck his head out from under the plush dragon.

"That was a close one," he whispered as the giant lass's arm encircled Pinky Dragon and caught him up in the hug.

"UUUUGH!" Wiglaf gasped as Grubella pulled Pinky—and him—closer. He could hardly breathe! He had to do something or Grubella would strangle him!

"Where is the key?" he rasped. "Pinky Dragon wants to know—where's the key?"

Grubella smiled in her sleep. She loosened her grip.

"SIWWY PINKY DWAGON!" she muttered. "YOU KNOW I KEEPS THE KEY UNDER MY PIWWOW!"

"Piwwow?" Wiglaf repeated, confused.

"Under her pillow!" Erica whispered hoarsely from the table.

"But she has so many pillows!" Angus groaned.

It was true. The bed was half-covered in pillows. Searching under all of them would be like hunting through the castle yard at DSA.

"I'll find it," said Dudwin. He jumped onto the bed and dove under the nearest pillow.

Wiglaf looked up at Worm. The dragon had pushed his snout up against the bars. He was snuffling, with a hopeful look on his face.

After a moment, Dudwin's head came out

from between two pillows. "Found the key!" he cried.

"Shhhhhh!" everyone said.

Dudwin clapped his hands over his mouth. "Sorry!" he said.

Wiglaf made his way over the pillows to Dudwin. Janice, Angus, and Erica jumped down onto the bed. Together, they shoved the giant pillow aside.

And there was the key. It was made of brass, like the birdcage. It had a circle at one end, and a long, thin bar with two prongs at the tip. Like everything else in Grubella's room, the key was giant-size.

Janice snapped her gum. "Maybe we can lift it together."

The five gathered around the key. Janice managed to pick up her end, but just barely.

"Zounds, that's heavy!" Angus let go of his part.

"Let's try harder. We can do it..." said Erica.

But she didn't sound so sure.

"What about the feather, Wiggie?" said Dudwin.

"Yes!" said Wiglaf. He pulled the Quickening Quill from his belt.

"Wait," Erica said. "The key might want to go on holiday like the carpet. Let's tie it to us before you wake it up. That way we can make sure it does what we want."

Erica untied a pink ribbon from around Pinky Dragon's neck. She tied the ribbon tightly around the key and handed the ends of the ribbon to Wiglaf. He held them in one hand while he tickled the key with the other.

*"Tickle, tickle, how time flies,*
*I'm waking you up, so now ARISE!"*

As Wiglaf put the quill back in his belt the key began to quiver. Then it sprang up and shook itself from end to end, like a dog shaking off water.

"Key—" Wiglaf began. But that was as far as he got.

The key began leaping around the pillows. Wiglaf was so startled, he nearly dropped the ribbon, but he managed to hold on.

"Leggo!" yelped the key. "Leggo! Gotta go! Gotta go home!"

"Listen, key. It was me who woke you up," Wiglaf said, gripping the ribbons. "Help us. Then I'll let you go."

"Leggo! Leggo!" shouted the key. "Gotta go!" It bucked like a wild bronco. It started bouncing all around the pillow, with Wiglaf hanging on behind. This was worse than the carpet. Much worse.

"Leggo!" the key squealed. "Gotta go home!"

"Wiglaf, make it stop!" Erica whispered. "It's going to wake Grubella!"

Wiglaf nodded. On the next buck he pulled the ribbon toward him and grabbed onto the key itself.

"Leggo!" the key shouted. "Leggo! Leggo!"

It shook and bounced, trying to knock Wiglaf off. Wiglaf held tight and managed to wrap his legs around the key. The key bounded across the pillows toward the table. Wiglaf tugged on the ribbon, trying to steer it to the cage. He had never ridden a horse. Or even a pony. But he thought that this must be like riding a runaway steed.

Wiglaf's friends ran after him.

The key banged into the table.

*CRASH!*

"OWIE!" it squealed as it fell back onto Grubella's bed.

Grubella's eyes flew open.

"Wiglaf, look out!" Dudwin yelled. "The giant lass is awake!"

# Chapter 12

Trubella blinked her giant eyes.

She sat up and saw the DSA kids running across her pillows.

"AM I DWEAMING?" she said.

"Yes!" Angus called to her. "You're dreaming. Close your eyes!"

"I NOT DWEAMING," the giant lass cried. And then she screamed a giant scream: "EEEEEE-EEEEEEEEEEEEEEK!"

She began thrashing and kicking and yelling, "MOMMY! THEWE AWE CWEEPY, CWAWLY HUMANS IN MY BED! EEEEEWWWWWW!"

Erica and Janice dove for the table and scrambled up. Erica whipped the rope from her tool belt and hoisted up Angus and Dudwin.

Wiglaf was still riding the wild key. And the key was still bucking and jumping across the bedside table.

"MOMMY!" bellowed Grubella. "I SCAWED OF HUMANS!"

"*Carrrrefullll, Mmmooommmmy!*" Worm called to Wiglaf.

All at once, the key stopped bucking. Its pronged tip quivered as if it were sniffing something.

"Gotta go...gotta go—HOME!" the key squealed. And then it shot like an arrow toward the lock of the cage.

"*Whoooa?*" burbled Worm as the key hurtled toward him.

"Wiglaf, jump!" Angus cried.

Wiglaf jumped off just before the key slammed into the lock and turned. *CLICK!*

The cage door was open!

*CLICK!*

Now the key had locked it again.

*CLICK!*

Open!

*CLICK!*

Locked.

*CLICK!*

Wiglaf scrambled to his feet on the tabletop. He climbed up the bars of the cage, waited for the right *CLICK!* and, with all his might, pulled the cage door open.

Worm bounced out, grinning. He unfurled his wings.

Grubella's mouth opened in a huge wail. "NOOOOOOOO!! DON'T GO, PWINCESS SPAWKLE!"

The giant lass grabbed for Worm, knocking Pinky Dragon onto the floor.

Worm barely dodged Grubella's grasp. He took off from the table and flew up to the ceiling of Grubella's room, where he circled, calling, *"Mommmmmmy! Mommmmmmy!"*

Wiglaf heard footsteps!

Grubella's wailing had woken her giant mom.

"DARLING?" called Lady Whopping-Large as she pounded up the stairs. "ARE YOU HAVING A BAD DREAM?"

"Run!" cried Janice.

"But where?" cried Angus.

Wiglaf looked around in dismay. How were they going to get down to the floor? There wasn't time for the rope. It was too far to jump. And anyway, they'd never escape the castle with giants chasing them.

Just then Worm flew down and landed on the table. He folded his wings.

*"Hoppp on, Mommmy!"* the dragon cried. *"Hoppp, Sirrr. Allll hoppp!"*

Quickly the Worm Official Rescue Mission scrambled onto the dragon's back.

"NOOO!" cried Grubella. "YOU AWE *MY* DWAGON! YOU CAN'T FWY AWAY!"

"Fly, Worm! Fly!" Wiglaf called.

Worm flapped his wings like crazy. But he stayed on the table. The five were too heavy for him.

*THUMP THUMP THUMP!*

Lady Whopping-Large's footsteps grew louder and louder.

Grubella lunged across the table and grabbed for the flapping dragon. She missed, but the next time she'd get him.

"I'm jumping off!" Wiglaf cried.

*"Mommmy, nooooooooo!"* cried Worm. He flapped harder.

"Fly, Worm!" called Wiglaf. "Farewell, my dear dragon!"

And he slid off the dragon's back.

# Chapter 13

s Wiglaf slid off Worm, the dragon lifted into the air.

"PWINCESS SPAWKLE!" Grubella screamed. She grabbed at Worm's tail, barely missing it.

"Fly, Worm!" Wiglaf called from the tabletop. "Fly away!"

Worm flew higher, out of the giant lass's reach just as Grubella's giant mom burst into the room waving a flaming torch.

Wiglaf dove under a troll doll's skirt.

"GRUBELLA, DARLING?" said Lady Whopping-Large. "WHAT'S GOING ON? WHAT'S WRONG?"

Worm and his passengers were circling near the ceiling.

"UP THEWE, MOMMY!" Grubella pointed. "HUMANS AWE STEAWING MY DWAGON!"

"DON'T WORRY, DARLING!" Lady Whopping-Large cried. "I'LL GET YOU YOUR DRAGON. AND I'LL GET ME A TASTY SNACK!" She waved her torch at Worm and his passengers. Worm flew higher. Janice had to duck to keep from hitting her head on the ceiling.

Grubella kept screaming. Lady Whopping-Large climbed on a footstool to better reach the humans.

With both giants busy with Worm, Wiglaf dashed out of his hiding spot. He had an idea—and maybe it would work. He pulled the Quickening Quill from his belt and ran over to Pinky Dragon. He began tickling the toy and chanting:

*"Tickle, tickle, how time flies,*
*I'm waking you up, so now ARISE!"*

Pinky Dragon blinked its button eyes. It spread

its plush pink wings and flew straight to the giant lass.

Grubella stared at her airborne toy. "PINKY DWAGON?" she said.

"It's me!" cried Pinky Dragon. "Let's play tea party with all your dollies!"

"OH, YES, PINKY DWAGON!" cried Grubella, forgetting all about Worm and his rescuers. "TEA PAWTY!"

But Lady Whopping-Large did not forget. She poked her fiery torch at the dragon and the humans. "I'LL TOAST YOU!" she boomed. "I'LL ROAST YOU!"

"Yikes!" cried Angus. "My toes are getting scorched!"

Grubella's mother drew back her arm.

"Look out, Worm!" Janice yelled from the back of the dragon.

The giant heaved the torch into the air. The flames flew straight at Worm!

Worm went into overdrive. He pumped his

wings and did a double flip, dodging the flames. The torch arched through the spot where Worm and WORM had been seconds before.

"MOMMY!" Grubella called. "WOOK! PINKY DWAGON HAS COME AWIVE!"

Lady Whopping-Large glanced at her daughter and her live plush toy. "THAT'S NICE, PRECIOUS," she called. "HAVE I EVER FIXED YOU TORCH-FRIED HUMANS?" She picked up the flaming torch and heaved it again.

But by now Worm had found his power. He dodged the torch easily with a triple loop-the-loop, and then did a nosedive straight down to his mommy.

Wiglaf grabbed onto Worm's tail. Worm flapped up again. Janice held Wiglaf by the belt while he scooted up Worm's tail and held on tight.

Lady Whopping-Large picked up her torch and took a swing at the flying dragon, but she missed by a mile.

Worm flapped toward a slit in the castle wall. Wiglaf and his friends ducked down and—*WHOOSH*! They were outside! Flying through the night sky!

Below, they heard Lady Whopping-Large roaring:

> "FIE FO FEE FOAM!
> WAIT'LL LORD WHOPPING-LARGE
> GETS HOME!
> FI FO FUM FEE!
> HE WILL CATCH YOU, YES, SIRREE!"

"Oh, go blow your nose, Whopping-Large!" Erica yelled.

"Go eat leech pond scum!" Wiglaf called from his seat on the tail section. He grinned. They had escaped. And Worm was safe!

"Woo-hoo!" shouted Janice. "That was the coolest battle ever!"

*"Wheeeeeee!"* burbled Worm. *"Taaaanks, Mommmy! Nottt likkke livve in cagge. Wannnnn ttto ssssee Brrrr Dave!"* He sneezed once more—

*AH-CHOOOOOO!*—nearly throwing off his passengers.

Worm flew WORM out of the Kingdom of Gigantia.

As he flapped over the Dark Forest, Wiglaf saw something fluffy and yellow floating toward the ground. He put a hand to his belt. Surekill was there. But the Quickening Quill was gone.

For once, Zelnoc had been right. The quill was just the thing for saving Worm. He hoped Zelnoc wouldn't be mad that he had lost it. And that Zizmor wouldn't be too upset that somewhere a carpet was flapping away on holiday. A giant brass key was clicking away in its lock. And a plush pink dragon was making one giant lass very happy.

Worm flew until the sun came up.

"There's DSA!" cried Janice.

Worm landed in a field. *"AHHH-CHOOO!"* he sneezed.

"Fly to Brother Dave, Worm," Wiglaf said, patting his dragon. "He will take care of you. We'll meet you back at DSA."

"*Brrrrr,*" purred Worm. He waited while the DSA friends hopped off his back. Then he spread his wings and flew straight for the DSA library.

"What'll we tell Uncle Mordred when we come back with no gold?" Angus asked Wiglaf as WORM started walking toward DSA.

"The truth," said Wiglaf. "The dragon in Hermit's Hovel didn't have any gold."

"Uncle Mordred will be mad," said Angus. "But then, he's always mad."

"Who says we don't have any gold?" said Dudwin.

"What do you mean, Dud?" asked Wiglaf.

"Spill," Erica commanded.

Dudwin grinned. He reached under his tunic and pulled out a gold chain. Dangling from it was a tiny gold crown charm.

"That's the giant doll's bracelet!" said Wiglaf.

"Yep." Dudwin nodded.

"Dud, you *stole* it!" Wiglaf said. "That makes you

no better than the giants!"

"Wait, that necklace looks familiar," Erica said. "Does the charm have any writing on it?"

Dudwin turned the crown over and read: "*To Queen Barb. Love, Kenny Boy.*"

"I thought so," Erica said. "That necklace belongs to my mother!"

Dudwin grinned. "It's not really stealing if they stole it from somebody else in the first place."

"You must give it back to the queen, Dud," Wiglaf said.

"Oh, Mumsy has a million gold necklaces," said Erica. "She won't care if Dudwin keeps this one."

"See, Wiggie?" Dudwin said. "I can keep it!"

"Or you *could* give it to Uncle Mordred," Angus said.

"It *would* make Mordred happy," Janice said.

"All right," said Dudwin with a sly grin. "If you promise I can come on your next adventure with you."

"Works for me," said Erica. "Your climbing

helped us."

"You're a cool dude, Dud!" said Janice. "Here, have a stick of gum."

"Thanks!" said Dudwin eagerly.

Wiglaf smiled. Maybe his not-so-little brother wasn't so bad. After all, he was a good climber. And he'd found a treasure for Mordred.

"We did what we set out to do," said Erica. "We saved Worm from the KNC dragon slayers."

"And from being Grubella's pet," said Angus.

"Mission accomplished!" cried Wiglaf as they ran across the DSA drawbridge and back to their school.